Brenna Lyons

Unexpected
Daddy

Fireborn Publishing Copyright Statement

PUBLISHER

Dedication

To Beth M... Slow down and let the baby get dirty. There's always a bath later.

My children, who teach me almost as much as I teach them.

Chapter One

Joey Biers sprinted through the ER doors and to the desk. "Jeremy and Alison Biers," he panted out.

"If you'll have a seat, Mister—"

"They said it was an emergency."

She shot him a look that said Joey was an idiot.

"I know everything here is technically an emergency, but—"

"If you'll just take a seat, sir," she suggested. "I'll see what I can find out for you."

The urge to pound his fist into the desk was overridden by the fact that he wouldn't learn anything about his brother and sister-in-law while sitting in a jail cell. Joey swallowed his pride and murmured his acceptance. That settled—for the moment—he ambled to the closest empty seat and all but collapsed into it.

The mad dash across town, coupled with a long day at the office, had taken its toll on him. Joey waited long enough to see the secretary at the desk dialing the phone before he closed his eyes and laid his head back on the cement block wall.

Sounds became muted, and he drifted in a semiconscious state. Rushing feet and announcements faded into the background. If it weren't for the acrid smells of sickness and antiseptics, he would surely have fallen asleep almost immediately.

As it was, it seemed he sat there for an inordinately long time. He was on the verge of going back to the desk to ask for an update, when a soft, female voice spoke from very close to him.

"Mister Biers?"

Joey levered his eyelids up and took stock of her. The doctor wasn't much older than his own twenty-six years, he'd wager, a petite brunette that would have been just his twin's type a few years ago.

Before he met Alison. "Yes. I'm Joey Biers."

"If you'd come with me, please." She turned without waiting for an answer and led the way through the double doors into the treatment area.

Joey tried hard not to peek into any of the alcoves. She would stop at whichever one was important to him, and the misery of others was none of his business.

It wasn't until they stopped at the elevator that he started to question where they were going. "They've been admitted?" Why hadn't anyone told him that? How bad were their injuries?

Bad. They said it was an emergency and I shouldn't waste time.

The doctor surged through the parting elevator doors and punched a button, forcing Joey to follow her. The doors closed them in.

"Doctor, I don't mean to be rude, but I want some answers."

She didn't look at him. "I know you do. You'll have to forgive me for being at a loss. One of the plus sides to going into obstetrics is not having to give bad news often. I'm... a little out of practice."

Obstetrics. Alison was a month from her due date. "Did they lose the baby? Or did something happen to Alison?" It was out before he had a chance to brace himself for what might be said.

No matter which member of his family Jeremy had lost, his brother would be crushed. *If he's lost them both, I don't think he'll survive it.*

The doctor looked up at him, her brown eyes tired and soulful. "There was an accident."

"Yes. The police said that." A drunken driver had run his brother's car into a ditch. Both Jeremy and Alison had been severely injured. *What a lousy thing to tell someone over the phone. Just that and nothing more.*

"Your brother managed to get his wife out."

"Alison." For some reason, it was important that the doctor use her name. Joey couldn't say what difference it made, but it made one.

"Alison. Yes..." She fidgeted and looked away for a moment. When she looked back, she'd steeled her expression.

The elevator doors opened, but neither of them moved. The doctor pressed the button to keep them where they were.

"Your brother didn't make it out of the wreckage alive. He got tangled in the seatbelt and...there was water in the ditch."

He drowned. The mental image sent shivers down Joey's spine. He nodded dumbly. Alison was going to be distraught. It was definitely the wrong time for that.

The doctor exited the elevator, and Joey followed her. For a moment, they walked in silence.

"How is Alison?"

She didn't answer immediately.

Finally, the doctor stopped and turned to look at him again. "Her injuries were too severe. I'm sorry. We tried everything."

His head in a flat spin, Joey tried to control his anger. "Why did you bring me up here if there's nothing left?" he snapped.

3

Her flitting hand movement drew Joey's eyes toward the huge plate glass window. Two rows of clear plastic bassinettes sat in the center of the room, all but a few of them occupied with tiny newborns.

Before he could question if one of them was his niece or nephew, the doctor pressed a buzzer and stated his last name.

Our last name. My gods, there's a baby in there who has no one else now. He or she depends on me.

One of the hovering nurses nodded and plucked a baby from the closer row. She turned toward the window, holding a swaddled infant with a pink knitted cap. Golden curls, which matched his own and Jeremy's, poked around the edges of the cap.

Tears burned at Joey's eyes. "A girl. She's... Is she okay?"

A smile flirted with the doctor's lips. "She's perfect, but we'll be keeping an eye on her for a few days." She paused for a moment. "Alison named her Abigail. Abigail Juliet Biers."

"Abby." It had been the forerunner in the name race, he knew. Joey stared at her, his heart pounding. *I don't know how to take care of a baby, but I guess I better learn quickly.*

"I have to ask you this," the doctor hedged.

Joey peeled his gaze away from his niece and focused it on the squirming doctor, warning bells going off in his head. "Ask me what?"

"Do you feel you can care for Abigail?" She shifted, as if in discomfort. "There are alternatives—"

"Not a chance. Abby stays with me." After the years he and Jeremy spent in foster care, there was no way

4

strangers were going to take his niece away from the family. *I'm not much family, but family comes first.*

She didn't second guess him. Her smile was wide and heartfelt. "In that case, I should probably introduce you to the nursery staff. If you need help, the nurses would be glad to show you the basics of baby care."

His heart eased a notch. "Thanks. That would be great." *Thank goodness. I don't have to do this alone.*

Chapter Two

Five weeks later

Abby stretched in the front carrier, and Joey faltered, placing a hand behind her. As many times as she did that, it was still hard to accept that she wasn't going to topple out of the carrier. Yet again, he wished there were straps at the shoulders to hold her in.

Car seats have them. Why don't front carriers? What if I trip or something?

He stopped and took a calming breath. *The nurses are right. I have to calm down and trust that competent care will be enough. I'll worry myself into an early grave this way.*

Joey winced. It was a thought he didn't want to consider. If something happened to him, Abby would be sent into foster care. "Don't worry, kiddo. I won't let that happen to you."

With that, he double checked the address and pushed through a gate into the home daycare. The only mark of what lay within was a computer-generated sign in the front window. There was a second four-foot fence that surrounded the backyard and separated it from the front. Joey ambled toward the gate.

He couldn't see the whole yard and didn't feel he should wander around a daycare unaccompanied. There were a few climbing structures and a sandbox. The latter wasn't covered, but the kids might be coming right back to it. Joey dismissed his concerns.

For now.

It wasn't as easy to dismiss the fact that there was no lock on either gate. *There isn't anything to keep kids from scaling the fence or opening the latch and walking away. What if she gets called away to the phone or to change a diaper?*

Of course, Abby can't climb yet, but it won't be long until—

Stop! If he didn't stop nitpicking, he was never going to find suitable childcare. *And I only have a week left to do it.* Work had been more than understanding about rolling 'maternity' and grieving together into a neat little six-week break, but he had to be able to return to work at the end of it.

"And I can't take you to work with me." Joey had to give the woman a chance. If she wasn't suitable, she wasn't, and the search would go on.

That settled, he went to the front door and knocked. There was no answer. He knocked harder. Still no answer.

"If you're looking for Sharon, don't waste your time," a strange female voice called out.

Joey turned and evaluated the woman peering over the fence from the next yard. *Just your average suburbanite, like the ones in the houses neighboring Jeremy and Alison's house. My neighbors now.*

She made a comment. I should answer her. "I had an appointment with her."

She snorted, rolling her dark eyes and fluffing her short, brown hair with a manicured hand. "Ten years ago, I would have told you this wasn't like her, but these days..." She sighed. "Most of the parents end up pulling when she flakes on them a few times."

The cynical part of Joey wanted to know what she had against Sharon. The rational half reminded him that Sharon wasn't here for their appointment.

He nodded to her. "Thanks for the information." The street beckoned. *The street and the continuing search.*

"Cute baby," she called after him.

Joey managed an honest smile and thanked her before turning toward his car. He closed the front gate and fished his keys out of his pocket.

Halfway down the block, a catcall stopped Joey short.

"What have we here? A gay boy with a baby."

The rainbow key tag. Fuck me! A glance back at the brute heading his direction had Joey revising that thought. *So not my type, even if he wasn't a homophobe.*

His decision to keep moving and ignore the resident bigot ended in a quiet death of misery at the second voice.

"How does a gay boy like you get a baby? You duped some woman into thinking you were straight long enough to have a kid with her?"

"No," the one behind him inserted. "Probably a sperm donor for his lesbo buddies, and they decided they didn't want a baby later. Then again, gay boy here is probably more maternal than the lesbos would have been."

Joey tried to round the one blocking him from his car, and his tormenter sidestepped to block the way again.

"So... Are you Mommy or Daddy?" He sneered, shooting an acid look up and down Joey's body.

Joey ground his teeth. He didn't want Abby in the middle of a fight, but these guys looked like that's what they were planning.

I could deny being gay. Say the keys are my brother's. Though it went against his nature, Abby was a good enough reason to do it. *Family comes first. Always.*

Joey opened his mouth to spout the lie, hoping that he didn't choke on the words, hoping harder than that they'd buy it.

"Hey, Joe. Get your ass in here," a voice called from his right.

Surprised, he looked around and spotted the man on the closest porch. Six feet or so of muscle, with his thumbs hooked in his front pockets, he didn't look happy at all. Dark brown hair with heavy streaks of gray over the ears formed a shaggy mane around a hard face. His shoulders were tensed, reinforcing the impression of a lion preparing to pounce.

The two hecklers took a step back, and Joey considered running for it. Something in the older man's expression nailed his feet to the cement.

I don't know who he is, but I get the feeling I'm safer with him than giving these two morons my back while I strap Abby into her car seat.

****

Geoff tore his gaze from the kid with the baby strapped to his chest and glared at Mark Jamison and his tag-along brother, Taylor. "We don't have a problem here. Do we, boys?" If he honestly believed pounding a lesson into the duo would work, they'd both have swallowed teeth already.

Mark took a second step away from the blond newcomer and waved his hand with a slight tremor. "No trouble, Geoff."

"Good. Because I could have sworn I told you I wouldn't stand for that sort of talk on my property."

Technically, none of them were on Geoff's property, but it was close enough for horseshoes, hand grenades, and thermonuclear weapons, he supposed. *And they know I won't put up with this. Especially not two on one...and not with a child involved, let alone a baby.*

"Just showing the man to his car," Taylor lied.

"Why would you do that? I'm sure good old Joe was just getting something *out* of the car before he came in for a visit."

He focused on the young man again. He was slim, not a match for the two Cro-Mag types he was facing. *Not that he appears to be looking for a fight.* If anything, he looked like he would bolt at the first opportunity. *It's a miracle that he hasn't done it already.*

Geoff hoped the kid was older than he looked, because he'd lay odds at just over legal drinking age. He had an angelic quality about him. *Probably all those blond curls and big, blue eyes.*

Twenty years ago, he would have been just my type.

He scowled. *Twenty years ago, I was still denying that I was gay and ruining a bunch of lives.*

Geoff swallowed to wet his throat. "Isn't that so, Joe?"

The blond hesitated for a moment, cleared his throat, and answered. "Yeah. Sure. I was just getting the diaper bag."

"Well get it and get your ass in here. Dinner is going to get cold."

He nodded and turned toward his car. Taylor moved to give him more room.

"Oh, and boys..." Geoff called for the brothers' attention. "You just make sure Joe doesn't come out to find any...accidents to his car. I *might* take that personally."

'Joe' grabbed the diaper bag, hurried up Geoff's walk, and locked the car with his remote. As he passed Geoff, he offered a tense whisper of thanks.

In the background, Mark clapped Taylor on the back, and they sauntered away.

One of these days, those two are going to do something stupid. Not for the first time, Geoff realized he didn't want to be within miles of here when it happened.

The worst of the confrontation momentarily avoided, he closed himself into the house and turned to talk to the young man he'd just aided.

'Joe' was oblivious to Geoff's inspection. The young father was busy changing a spit-up encrusted sleeper. His movements weren't as smooth as Geoff would have expected, and his blue eyes followed every movement, as if it was still new to him.

The baby couldn't have been more than a month or so old, and though her dad was unsure, she seemed perfectly at home with his handling. To Geoff, that meant the kid was a good father.

Chapter Three

Joey knew the man was watching his every move. That made him all the more nervous. "Thank you again for your help back there."

The older man leaned against the closed door. "So, why don't you tell me your name?"

A raw laugh escaped his lips. "Since you've been using my name..."

He tensed. "Your name really is Joe?"

"Well, most people call me Joey, but...yes. Joey Biers." Joey looked up at his host. "And yours?"

"Geoff. Geoff Allread."

There was a moment of silence.

Joey used it to get Abby into a new sleeper. "I guess we should go now. We've been more than enough trouble to you."

"Not a good idea. I said you were here for dinner. If you leave right away—"

"It will be obvious you lied for us," Joey concluded.

Geoff grunted his agreement. "It's chili for dinner, if that's okay with you."

"Sure. I love chili." Even if he hadn't, Joey wouldn't have balked. He was intruding on Geoff's dinner. *Imposing on his life. Putting him in danger, most likely.* Even if, as he suspected, Geoff was gay, that didn't mean he made a habit of intervening in hate crimes.

The man in question pushed off the door and walked past Joey and Abby. "Why don't you bring that little lady and come into the kitchen?"

Joey hesitated only a moment and then trailed behind Geoff. Abby wobbled in his arms, trying to hold herself upright without his assistance.

Geoff glanced up from the heavenly-smelling pot simmering on the stove. "How old is she?"

"Five weeks. I don't know where the time went."

"If you won't think I'm rude for asking?" Geoff hinted.

Joey sighed. "You want to know how someone like me ended up with a baby."

"Oh, it happens often enough, but I highly doubt you ended up with this little one the same way I ended up a father." There was a bite of something bitter in that.

"You're a father?" It was out before Joey could censor himself. "Uh...sorry. That was rude." His cheeks flamed.

Geoff shrugged. "As you saw outside, life is rude." He paused for a moment. "I tried the marriage route. Had a beautiful little girl. Ryssa."

"And you came out?" It was one of the oldest stories around, after all.

"Eventually. When my daughter was a teenager and I foolishly thought she would understand. But we're talking about how you ended up with that little beauty now."

"My brother and his wife were killed in an accident. Drunk driver. That leaves me to raise Abby. Not that I'm looking for a way out. Abby is as close as I'll ever come to having a child, I'm sure." *Stop it.* He was rambling.

I blame it on lack of sleep. Abby still hadn't figured out day from night, it seemed.

"The car seat?"

"What?" That pseudo question made no sense that Joey could fathom.

Geoff put the lid on the pot and turned toward him. "The car seat saved Abby? I mean, that's what they're designed to do."

The question reopened wounds Joey had been too busy to obsess over much. He forced the words out in something that might pass for an even voice. "Alison was pregnant. She lived long enough for the doctors to do the C-section, but not much longer than that."

His host winced. "That would make for a lousy night for the entire family."

A wry smile pulled up at one side of Joey's lips. He motioned between himself and Abby. "This is the entire family."

****

Geoff watched Joey out of the corner of his eyes as the young man fed his niece a bottle. Though he feigned interest in the ball game on television, he couldn't have recounted the score if asked.

Joey had tried to make a graceful exit after dinner, but Abby had decided the tank was empty. *Babies come first.*

After all these years, the longing to be a father was still as potent as ever. Having one in the house was damned close to torture.

Bury it. That time is over, and I'll never be a father again.

Abby released the nipple and started to fuss.

Gas. Geoff didn't question it. *Once you learn the difference in a baby's cries, you never forget it.*

Right on cue, Joey set the bottle down on the coffee table, raised Abby to his cloth-covered shoulder, and started to burp her. After several long, tense moments, he'd only released a little bit of the whopper that was surely brewing in the baby's stomach.

Geoff gave up all pretenses and stared at him. "Having problems?"

"It's the one thing I've never been good at," he admitted.

"There's a trick to it."

Joey met his gaze solidly. "Mind sharing it?" There was a hint of a plea in that.

"Sure." His voice came out gruffer than he would have liked, but Geoff put his hands out for the baby.

She was lighter than Geoff could remember Ryssa being at birth, let alone at this age. Still, Abby felt right in his arms, as his own daughter had so long ago.

Get on with it. Abby isn't mine. She's Joey's, and they both need help learning a few things.

Geoff cupped his hand low on Abby's back and started thumping lightly up her spine. When he reached her shoulders, he started at the bottom again. "Just work the gas up a few times, and—"

Right on cue, the baby let out a deafening belch.

He chuckled. "Been holding out on Uncle Joey, have you?" he teased her.

The uncle in question was silent for a few minutes. "You're good with her."

"Once you learn, you never forget," Geoff dismissed him. Oh, but it did feel good to hold a baby again.

"Ever considered taking care of a baby?"

Geoff startled at the suggestion. He gaped at Joey for a minute. "You're kidding, right?"

"You said you'd been laid off, if I recall?"

"Yes, but—"

"And your unemployment is running out soon. In this economy, finding another job may be hard."

It has been. Impossible, it seems.

Why the hell did I tell him that? Talking to Joey was just so easy, and it had been a long time since Geoff had had someone to talk to. "That's true. But... I know this hasn't escaped your notice, Joey. I'm a guy."

He laughed heartily. "You're stuck in stereotypes?"

Geoff's face flushed, and he cleared his throat. "Well...no. It's not that I'm saying I can't do it. Won't you be uncomfortable having a male babysitter?"

"I'm not stuck in stereotypes, either. And considering the nightmares I've seen so far... You're good with her. You've done this before, too." Joey sounded far too serious.

He fought for a rational answer.

"I need someone good with Abby. You're certainly that. That's the number one requirement for a nanny or babysitter, isn't it?"

As if in confirmation, she snuggled into Geoff's shoulder.

Joey hurried on. "I probably can't pay you what you're used to, but it'll be something, and with unemployment running out, something is better than nothing. If you find a job later that you want to take...well, I'd just ask for a couple of weeks to find someone else to take care of Abby."

Geoff was tempted, but... "I don't have any baby equipment," he blurted out. Even purchasing it secondhand would be expensive.

Joey shot a glance at the door. "I don't really like the neighborhood. No offense to you."

It's not all bad. Tricia Price and her mother were absolute gems, and most of his other neighbors were a nod and wave friendly. If it wasn't for the Jamison morons, it would be a downright cozy place to live.

"None taken. And you can see why this is a bad idea." The last thing he wanted to do was expose Abby to the Jamisons. But Geoff's heart sank, all the same.

"Not really. I can see why it would be worth it to add in gas money so you can take care of her at our home."

His certainty stunned Geoff. "You're serious about this. Aren't you?"

"Give me one good reason why I shouldn't be?" He hesitated a moment, and his expression lost its spark.

Geoff had the insane urge to reach out and comfort him. Stifling it was more difficult than he wanted to admit. Even to himself.

"I will consider an answer of 'not interested' as a valid reason why you shouldn't consider it."

The words stuck in Geoff's throat. He'd been worried about what he'd do when the unemployment ran out. He'd been faced with the choice of trying to find work in fast food or retail at forty-three years old. No matter what Joey paid, it would probably be better than minimum wage.

And a hell of a lot more enjoyable than asking if the customer wants fries with that. "What time should I get there?"

Joey's smile made Geoff's heart stutter and his cock stir.

Oh, this does not bode well. Though, he couldn't say why he'd think that.

Chapter Four

Six days later

Geoff lifted the carrier from Abby's car seat, leaving the base belted into his truck. Joey had purchased a car seat to allow Geoff to take the baby shopping with him...or to the park or the doctor's office.

It was the safest on the market, of course. Geoff didn't doubt that Joey had agonized over safety reports online for days before he chose the model he ultimately bought. He didn't doubt it, because Joey had purchased two of them and prematurely retired the model Alison and Jeremy had purchased during Abby's pregnancy.

These new carrier-car seats were an ingenious design. In addition to those uses, they also hooked onto strollers and shopping carts. Yet again, Geoff marveled at the luxury of modern childcare.

The carrier secured on the shopping cart, Geoff pushed the very alert and interested Abby down the first aisle. Talking to her about what they were doing was a natural extension.

Not in baby talk, of course. That only taught children to speak poorly. He'd explained it to Joey, who'd reluctantly agreed it was best to speak properly to a baby, though movies and television were littered with baby-talking idiots.

His joking comment about her Uncle Joey's insistence on using the "best rated" brand of disposable diapers was cut short by a woman's voice.

"Your granddaughter is absolutely adorable."

Geoff turned to look at her, stunned by the pronouncement. *I don't look that old, do I?*

The thirty-something continued on, oblivious to his reaction. Baby talk spewed from her lips in a sickening show. As if in reaction, Abby screwed up her face in a pout that Geoff was certain indicated her readiness to scream.

"I bet you're granpa's pwecious little sweetie. Awen't you just?"

"She's not my...uh...not my granddaughter."

The woman's cheeks darkened in a blush. "I'm sorry. I just assumed. She's your niece?" she ventured. Clearly, she was having problems imagining that.

"Yeah." It was close enough. *And a hell of a lot better than saying I'm Abby's nanny.* "I'm watching her for my...brother." And why did it feel so wrong to say that?

Her smile would have devastated most men his age, and Geoff understood the descriptor of a baby as a "chick magnet" for the first time in his life.

"Well, she is a little heartbreaker," she imparted. With that, she was gone, wheeling her cart through the sparsely-populated aisle.

For a moment, Geoff stared after her, confused by his reactions.

If he was having so much trouble admitting he was taking care of Abby as a job, did that mean he was too involved with Joey and Abby? That he was starting to think of his involvement as something other than a job? Maybe something permanent?

One look at Abby's big blue eyes convinced him that there was no such thing as 'too involved'. She chewed on two fingers and stared at him with blue eyes that closely matched her uncle's, seemingly waiting for the running commentary to continue.

If I'm that self-conscious about this job, maybe I should look for something in construction or manufacturing again. That thought in mind, Geoff ambled down the aisle, grabbing formula and other necessities he knew were on Joey's list.

Always a month ahead of what Abby will need. At least. Joey was the parental form of a survivalist.

Never mind that. I'm avoiding the subject again.

Should I go back to work? Going back to my usual work doesn't mean I can't be friends with Joey and Abby. It doesn't mean I can't babysit just to do it.

The security mirror at the end of the aisle caught his attention, and Geoff surveyed his reflection. He was still solidly built, but he was definitely showing his age. The gray in his hair and creasing skin made no secret of the fact that Geoff would never see the preferred side of forty again.

Of course, that was probably part of the problem he'd been having with finding another job. Mastery of his craft had taken a back seat to salary concerns in the current economic climate. An employer could hire three—nearly four—fresh-faced kids, newly graduated from the local vo-tech, for less than they'd pay two men with Geoff's experience.

Experience? Just say it. I'm getting old.

That put a pall on the outing, and Geoff mulled over his problems and the options—slim as they were—available to him for solving them.

At the checkout, he stopped to stare at the daily paper. *Nanny or carpenter? Which should I focus on?*

Nanny will pay the bills in the short term, but being a carpenter that isn't day labor will provide medical. There was no way Joey could afford to do that.

He touched the paper, resigned to the fact that he would have to seek a position in industry.

Abby yawned widely, and he smiled. The thought of not seeing her every day sent an ache through his chest.

"Give an old man two more weeks to think about it?" Geoff teased Abby. *Anything to keep from making the obvious choice today.*

As if in answer, she waved her hand at him and smiled.

Chapter Five

Three weeks later

Geoff looked up at the sound of the front door opening. When Joey didn't immediately appear, he set the book he'd been reading down on the coffee table and headed into the front hall.

Joey stood, his back to the door, as if he was holding off hordes. Geoff didn't question that he was weary. While Geoff got to go home every night, Joey worked a full day and then came home to baby duty at night.

Geoff had extended his work day into making dinner for the two of them every night, and he did light housework while Abby slept or played in the swing, but the nighttime feedings were murder when you had no one to take turns with.

Day after day, he'd watched Joey use coffee to keep himself moving. Nine weeks into his unexpected fatherhood—a situation that was thankfully usually shared by two people who could spell each other—Joey was in zombie mode. His blue eyes were shadowed with dark circles, and he needed sleep.

Geoff went to his side, took Joey's briefcase, and set it on the foyer table. "Let's get you into a hot bath, kid."

Joey groaned deeply. "Need to have dinner first."

"I'll bring it up. Look, either you're getting in that tub, or I'm putting you there and bathing you." Though he kept it light, saying it was enough to render his cock hard and heavy behind his zipper.

Joey's eyes opened, and he looked up at Geoff with longing. The urge to slant his mouth over Joey's and end this maddening arousal was difficult to shake. *Do that again, kid, and I'll do something that will keep you awake for hours.*

"Which will it be?" Geoff challenged.

"Bath." But he didn't say whether he'd rather be bathed or bathe himself.

Good thing. He needs to eat. If Geoff got started now, that wouldn't be happening anytime soon.

"Can you make it up there on your own, or do you need a little help?"

That look of longing persisted, but Joey shook his head in the negative. "No. I can make it up there."

"Okay then...get going."

Though he knew he should head to the kitchen, Geoff watched Joey making his way up the stairs. Yeah, the kid was young. He had that sweet, tight ass thing going for him.

Which isn't going to put food down in front of either of us. Geoff retreated to the kitchen with a sigh.

****

Joey trudged into the hall bathroom upstairs and started shedding clothing, cursing himself silently as a half dozen types of fool. Yes, he was tired, but apparently he was so tired he was imagining things.

Geoff was an old man.

Well, not old, precisely. What did you call a man in his forties and not come off as insulting? Seasoned? Mature? He was too tired to continue the search for an appropriate word.

He called Joey 'kid' often enough to let Joey know that Geoff didn't see him as a potential lover. Obviously, Geoff felt Joey was too young for him.

And maybe I am, but it's been a long damn time, and Geoff makes my tired body stand up and take notice. If he thought Geoff was seriously interested in getting into his bed, Joey would make it clear there were no barriers to it.

He hesitated with one shoe off, his muddled mind following that thought to the realities of the situation. *There are no barriers on my side, but there might be for Geoff. Technically speaking, I'm his boss. It's likely a line he won't want to cross.*

Joey peeled off his other shoe and dropped it more forcefully than was called for. *Yeah, I'm tired. I'm going to get a hot bath, eat some dinner, wish Geoff a good night, and try to get a few hours of sleep before Abby wakes up for a feeding.*

****

Joey was just getting out of the tub when Geoff brought the tray of food up for him. Drying his legs gave Geoff a heart-stopping view of the kid's glorious ass and a peek at the equipment hanging between his legs.

That quickly, his cock went from half mast to aching readiness again. *Fuck. The kid is going to keep my heart in an aerobic state, for sure.*

Joey straightened and turned. There was no move to cover himself, no jump or blush at finding Geoff behind him. He panned his gaze down to Geoff's crotch, and Joey's cock followed suit.

Not yet. He can't keep pushing himself this way. "In bed, kid. You need to eat before you fall on your face."

"Not sure I'm hungry," Joey whispered, still staring at Geoff's cock as if he'd devour it, given the chance.

Not now, he reminded himself. But his body had other ideas.

Fuck this. Geoff set the tray on the sink and took the two steps that brought them together. Placing one hand at the back of Joey's head, Geoff crushed their mouths together.

Their lips parted, and Geoff moaned at the heat between them. He'd had lovers before, of course, but they had been hookups he'd used to scratch an itch. Something told Geoff this wouldn't be anything like the others.

Their mouths meshed, and one of Joey's arms circled Geoff's neck. The opposite hand went to work on his jeans, yanking Geoff out of daydreams where he tossed Joey on the nearest bed and fucked him until they were both senseless.

Geoff backed off a step. "Food first," he insisted.

The hand at his crotch stroked expertly up and down the column of Geoff's ready cock. "Eating is definitely an option."

The invitation in his voice had Geoff on the edges of something fierce and uncompromising. "Nutritious food first," he qualified. "After that..." He stroked his hips to drive his cock against Joey's hand.

"But—"

"I'm not reheating dinner." Geoff stopped short of saying he wasn't stopping what he planned for after dinner. It was up to Joey to take that in context...or not.

Joey opened his mouth to answer.

"Eat. Now."

He nodded, grabbed the tray, and headed for his bedroom, stark naked and appealing.

Fuck. He's going to give me a coronary that way.

****

Joey put his fork down, and Geoff shot him another warning look. "I'm full. Honest. You put enough food on that plate for two."

"And I'm sure you ate lunch today." His sarcasm said he knew the answer before Joey had a chance to react to it.

He set the tray on the end table, trying to hide the blush rising in his cheeks.

"Thought so," Geoff inserted. "Do I have to start packing you lunches, too?"

The thought of it warmed Joey, but he tried not to show it. Yes, he was a sappy romantic, and that sounded *wayyyy* too domestic. Since that was probably not the way Geoff meant it, Joey had to get his mind off of daydreams of something permanent.

At any time, the two week notice flag will go up and he'll find a job in his own field. What would happen then? Would they promise to remain friends? Actually get together a few times? *Probably not much more than that,* he conceded. That was a disheartening thought, if Joey had ever had one.

"Joey?"

He pasted on a weak smile. "Just tired, I guess."

Geoff nodded and started to rise from the mattress.

"So, I guess we shouldn't waste time talking, huh?" Joey hurried to add, his heart thundering at the idea that Geoff might be considering leaving. *We had a deal...sex after I ate. He isn't backing out now, is he?*

Geoff's determined expression said that was the last thing he intended. His muscled body sank to the mattress again, and his hand cupped the back of Joey's skull.

The kiss was no less involved than the one in the bathroom had been, and Geoff didn't balk when Joey unbuttoned his jeans. If anything, that stepped the heat up a few notches.

Geoff broke off the kiss and shot Joey a crooked smile. "What's your preference?"

"Bottom." He hoped that was agreeable to Geoff. Though Joey had given on occasion, he really enjoyed being on the receiving end of a hard fuck, and with as long as it had been for him, he really wanted that tonight.

Geoff's cock twitched behind his jeans. "Perfect."

Joey shivered in anticipation.

"Do you have supplies?" Geoff continued.

He nodded and turned to the nightstand to retrieve the condoms and lube. His fingers went boneless, depositing them to the mattress at the sight of Geoff's open shirt being hiked out of his jeans and off his shoulders.

Damn, the man is ripped. Geoff was in incredibly good shape for his age. *Probably because of his chosen profession.* His chest and arms were muscular, with just a hint that love handles might be in his future.

The shirt hit the floor, and Joey took a moment to appreciate the dusting of gray-shot curls on Geoff's chest, in stark contrast to the nearly hairless expanse of his own.

27

It couldn't hold his attention long. Not with the zipper on Geoff's jeans sliding down and revealing the deep red underwear beneath.

Not boxers. Joey wondered if they were briefs or boxer briefs. He wasn't sure if he blinked as he waited to find out.

"You should breathe," Geoff taunted.

Joey scowled, still focused on the jeans slipping past Geoff's hips and down his thighs.

Boxer briefs. Yum. Underwear told you a lot about a guy, and boxer briefs nearly ensured a hot time in bed.

"Joey?"

"I'm breathing," he snapped.

"Since you're talking, I'm sure you are. Good thing, too. I wouldn't want you to pass out on me."

That's it. Though he didn't want to miss a minute of what was happening, Joey peeled his attention from Geoff's disrobing and glared at him.

A wicked little grin curved Geoff's lips, making Joey's heart stutter in excitement. "How long has it been?"

Joey's brain was mush. It took an inordinately long time to put the question into context and even longer to come up with an answer to it. "Five months. I think. Maybe six." He tried his best to calculate it. "Yeah. Six."

Geoff nodded solemnly in response. "We should probably take it slow then."

"You can't tell me slow is what you want after that kiss."

Chapter Six

Geoff's cock felt a size too large for his skin, and his mouth went dry. "You're saying you don't?" *If he doesn't, the gloves come off.*

"Hell no," he attested.

Getting his clothes off never seemed to take so long before. Geoff yanked his jeans and socks off together, then started pulling his underwear away.

It was clear he had Joey's complete attention. If the kid's shallow breathing and wide, innocent eyes weren't indication enough, the clear fluid leaking from the slit in his ram-hard cock would be.

Geoff had always thought of striptease as a game youngsters played, but there was something inherently appealing in watching Joey's reactions. Give him a peek, and Joey swallows hard or licks his lips. Take it away a bit, and hear him gasp, see him sway a bit toward you. Slide the underwear nearly to the base, and see his lips part.

Enough. "I believe you promised me something in the bathroom."

Joey didn't raise his head. "Did I?" He wasn't being coy. He was so rattled, Geoff wondered how much experience Joey had.

He made short work of the underwear and returned to the mattress, sidling up to Joey.

The kid wasted no time. He was chest to chest with Geoff in a heartbeat, his lips crushed to Geoff's.

It was heart stopping. Just when Geoff thought he'd nearly reached Nirvana, their cocks brushed. Joey pistoned his hips, causing the contact to repeat. Again. And again.

Joey's smooth hand circled Geoff's cock and started stroking. Though he racked his brains, Geoff couldn't recall ever having a hand that soft but masterful working him before.

Fuck! I could come like this far too easily.

No. There was a hell of a lot more Geoff wanted.

He broke off the kiss. "You *did* make a promise."

Joey nodded, his eyes half-lidded. "Sure." His hand still worked at Geoff's cock, nearly bringing him off the bed in pleasure.

"Eating?" he prompted Joey.

His eyes cleared a bit, and Joey looked down at the cock in his hand. "Oh yeah," he breathed.

At his hesitation, Geoff made the leap to the question Joey was surely working at. "I'm safe, but I don't bareback, if that's what you're worried about."

Joey turned and grabbed a condom from the nightstand. He ripped it open and tossed the packet in the general direction of the trash can.

The next few minutes were mind altering. *Damn but the kid can even make putting a condom on sexy.*

Before Geoff could find the words to comment on it, Joey's mouth was wrapped around Geoff's cock and making good on the promise.

His eyes may have looked innocent, but his mouth certainly wasn't. Geoff moaned at the skill of the blow job he was lucky enough to be getting. Joey created a suction that caved his cheeks inward and gave the illusion of being snug inside a tight hole.

His ass will be tighter. Geoff ran his fingers through Joey's silken curls. He trailed them down the smooth skin of Joey's back. He'd obviously been missing out by choosing men his own age for sex.

Joey took him to the root, and Geoff shuddered, stamping down the need to come. Ruthlessly.

"Enough," Geoff grumbled. He had to stop Joey, or neither of them would get what they'd clearly come into this liaison to get out of it.

Joey's expression announced his confusion and hurt, and Geoff forced his voice to soften.

"I intend to tap that sweet ass tonight. I think we can agree on that?"

Joey's cock slapped wetly against his stomach. "Yeah. Definitely."

"Then you're not finishing me with your mouth. Not yet, anyway."

That delicious little half-shiver worked its way over Joey's body again. That settled, Geoff reached for the lube.

****

Fuck me! This is going to be good.

Geoff worked the lube over his fingers and cock with practiced ease. That accomplished, he leaned forward and pressed his lips to Joey's chest. While his hands were rough and his hair thick and bristling, Geoff's lips were sinfully soft and inviting.

"Lay back," he ordered.

That confused Joey for a moment. His former lovers liked to come from the back.

"Life is just a series of new experiences. Relax and let them happen."

31

How many times had Jeremy said that, usually when Joey was obsessing over some insignificant, little thing? *Too many to count.*

Joey complied, spreading his legs and lifting his knees to accommodate Geoff.

Geoff's smile sent up a swarm of butterflies in Joey's stomach. The older man's finger, trailing around the ring of his anus slowly, set his heart on overdrive.

"Relax for me."

Is he kidding? How was he supposed to relax with every nerve ending in his body clamoring for more?

One finger inched in, and Joey gasped, his muscles ratcheting down to hold it tight. Geoff grunted and started working it in and out.

Just when Joey would have begged for more, he pulled back to the rim and returned with two fingers. Joey cried out sharply in response.

Geoff hesitated. "Too much?"

"Not enough."

A lazy smile lit his eyes, and Geoff worked him up with two fingers.

The first brush over his prostate had Joey bowing up off the mattress with a ragged shout. By the third, he realized he wasn't going to last much longer.

"Fuck, I'm going to—"

"Not without me."

The fingers disappeared, and his latex-covered cock pushed at the lubed opening. Joey pushed back, desperate for the climax so close at hand.

There was no play at working him up further. The instant Geoff was past the ridge of muscle, he thrust up, finding the already-sensitized prostate.

A moment of stillness followed. Geoff's hands stroking at Joey's rigid buttocks was almost more than he could stand.

His hands tightened on Joey's hips, and the first few strokes passed in a pleasant haze. Geoff groaned and started thrusting in earnest.

The rest was a blur of moving bodies and sounds of passion. Climax rolled up Joey's sac, through his cock, and erupted onto his stomach and chest.

He dimly noted a sound of appreciation from Geoff. Then Geoff was tensing, moving in short strokes, buried nearly to the hilt in Joey.

The effect set off violent aftershocks that curled Joey's toes. Literally. He'd never had a man cause that marked a reaction before.

In the aftermath, Joey was breathless, his mind muddled. Had he screamed? His raw throat seemed to attest he had.

Good thing the nurses taught me to acclimate Abby to noise. Sure, she'd never heard *those* noises, but noise was noise to an infant.

With Geoff around, she might hear a lot more of this. Something told Joey Geoff wasn't the type of man that would be content with sex once in a while.

For that matter, though he'd never had a problem with long periods of abstinence, Joey was sure having Geoff around would keep him hungry, as well.

They came down to Earth slowly, both of them panting and sweat-covered. Little whispers of motion taunted Joey with a ready supply of hot sex.

Joey moaned, pressing up to seat Geoff's cock deeper in his ass. Geoff's callused hands tightened on Joey's hips, and he levered himself farther inside, brushing Joey's prostate again in the process.

The crisp hairs bisecting Geoff's chest were tantalizing against his own. He'd suspected Geoff would be good in bed, but Joey hadn't expected it to be quite as scorching as it had been.

Neither of them offered comment. Joey wasn't certain he was able to yet. *Well, not making sense, anyway.*

Damn, that was good.

Abby's cry announced—good or not—it was over, and Joey sighed. *Over for the moment,* he amended silently.

Geoff eased out of Joey's ass, prompting a groan of protest. In the next moment, Geoff had peeled off the condom, dropped it in the bedside trash can, and left the bed.

"I'll get Abby. You need the rest."

"For more of you, I hope," Joey replied. He was too exhausted to add the seductive tone he'd intended.

Geoff's expression was hot in promise. "I don't think that's out of the question." Before Joey could form the words to answer, he was out the door, his jeans in hand.

Joey grabbed a handkerchief from the nightstand drawer and used it to clean up. Too tired to seek out the hamper, he tossed it to the floor and flopped back to the mattress.

A quick pit stop in the hall bathroom later, the half-dressed carpenter's voice wafted over the baby monitor. Geoff's tones were soothing, and Abby quieted almost immediately.

Joey closed his eyes, savoring the experience as if the words were meant for him and not for his niece. All told, Geoff was the best thing that had ever happened to him and Abby. The inner romantic was making plans to entice Geoff to stay on as a permanent addition to the household.

All the while, the rational side of his mind cautioned him against rushing things.

It's hard not to rush such a good *thing.*

Joey sighed, then surrendered to the lullaby of Geoff's crooning voice.

****

Abby gave it the old college try, and Geoff smiled at her determination to keep herself awake. One little fist rubbed at a closed eye. When her sucking tapered off to nothing, she would kick her feet and return to the chore with a passion... only to taper off again a few moments later.

Finally, she sighed. Her fist loosened, and her feet drew up to Geoff's chest. When her lips went slack and released the bottle, he knew she was down for a longer sleep.

He'd already changed her diaper at the burping break, so it was crib time. *An overly padded crib, but there's nothing wrong with that.* In that respect, Joey probably wasn't much different than many first-time parents.

Geoff veered toward Joey's bedroom to let him know he'd be back as soon as he emptied the bottle and rinsed it. He stopped and smiled.

Lack of sleep had caught up with Joey, and the young man was deeply asleep, his chest rising and falling in the slow cadence of dreamless slumber. He lay in a full sprawl, taking up most of the queen-sized bed, oblivious to everything around him.

Just what he needs. Food, sleep... Of course, the rest was something they'd both needed desperately, he'd wager.

Geoff wasn't certain how long Abby would sleep before her next feeding, and Joey needed at least one unbroken night of sleep. The answer was clear as a still lake. He would get his emergency bag from the truck and find somewhere distant enough in the house that Abby wouldn't wake her exhausted uncle up when she started crying for her next meal.

That plan in mind, he pulled the quilt from Joey's waist to his shoulders, collected Joey's dinner tray, turned off the light, and closed the door quietly behind himself.

Chapter Seven

Joey yawned at the blaring of the alarm clock next to his head. His hand connected with the snooze bar on the second swat, and he fumbled the switch into the off position in the deafening silence.

Every muscle in his body screamed at him to go back to sleep but his spoilsport mind reminded Joey that he had to go to work. It went on to amend that he had to get a shower, get dressed, get a cup of coffee, and check on Abby before Geoff—

Wide awake and his heart pounding, Joey listened for Abby over the baby monitor. There was nothing. Not a peep.

While he'd like to believe she'd slept through the night for the first time, his overactive imagination had other ideas. What if she'd stopped breathing? SIDS was more common in premature babies than other infants, and Abby wasn't only a preemie—she had been traumatized at birth.

That was as far as his rational mind made it before Joey leapt from the bed and bolted to the nursery. Seeing the crib empty didn't help his thundering heart rate, and his runaway mind started speculating on wild possibilities.

Stop! Just stop! Joey took a calming breath. The answer was simple, he was sure.

Geoff must have thought Joey needed the sleep and stayed the night to take care of Abby. He wouldn't have wanted the baby waking Joey, so he would have taken her somewhere else in the house.

Where? Probably the living room. Her travel playpen was down there, and it would be far removed from the bedrooms.

Fairly certain that his niece wasn't dead or kidnapped, Joey took the time to pull on a pair of pajama pants.

His trek toward the stairs stopped short at the sound of Abby babbling. One foot extended over the top riser, Joey turned his head to the right, away from the nursery and his room and toward the master bedroom that sat on the other side of the hall bath from Abby's room.

He wouldn't! But something told Joey Geoff had used the room.

Geoff doesn't know. But his anger was still raw and unreasoning.

Cork it. Just thank him for watching Abby and be subtle about the rest. That decided, Joey made his way into the master bedroom.

The room was the single most feminine room in the house, the room that felt most like Alison to him. As always, it put Joey in a state of awe. While the rest of the house had something of a masculine feel to it, this bedroom and the nursery were the exceptions to the rule. This room in particular—probably because it was an adult woman's space.

Since Joey was gay, there was no chance there would be a woman around as Abby's female role model. Always one to plan ahead, Joey had decided that keeping 'Alison's bedroom' as she'd left it would provide the connection his niece would one day need to a mother figure.

His heart stuttered at the sight of Geoff, the rough woodsmith asleep in the sleigh bed, surrounded by

Alison's laces and ruffles. There was a tearing sense of wrongness about it, though Joey couldn't find the words to explain it, even to himself.

That's because it's not rational. Knowing that didn't make it any less powerful.

Just get Abby and don't try to explain it until you find the words.

Her babbling drew his eyes to the bassinette at the bedside, and Joey rushed to it, gathering her into his shaking hands. He'd always hated the bassinette. It didn't look sturdy to him, and the nightmares he'd had the five nights until Abby came home from the hospital had convinced Joey to abandon the flimsy piece of furniture and move Abby directly into the crib.

Of course, he'd prepped that with all the bumpers—so she wouldn't get her leg or head caught between the upright slats—slats whose spaces were reportedly too narrow to allow that to happen anyway—and the smaller baby wrangler inside, so the terry cloth walls would keep her far from the crib-side padding and any chance of suffocation.

The nurses would say I'm rambling and being overprotective again. The nurses would be right, but that didn't stop Joey from doing these things. There was no one else to worry about Abby but him and no other family members for either of them.

It has to be me, and I will be the parent Alison and Jeremy would have been. So help me God! Abby won't want for anything I can provide.

"Joey? You okay?" Geoff rumbled out.

Answering him was difficult. Joey nodded, his mind and heart in a riot.

He sat up, his brow furrowed. "You sure? You look like you've seen a ghost."

That sent a flutter of nervous motion through his stomach. He'd lost everything but Abby, and ghosts were the last thing he needed reminding of.

"Yeah... Just... Just don't use the bassinette, okay?"

Geoff shot a look of confusion at the wicker and lace contraption. "Sure, but...why?"

"Just don't! Okay?" It came out harsher than Joey had planned, an order instead of a request.

"Sure."

Joey turned toward the hallway, his breathing rasping in his ears. "And don't use that room," he shot back.

Geoff's agreement was slower coming and seemingly wary.

It should be. My reaction wasn't called for.

But that didn't stop Joey from stomping down to the nursery and slamming the door behind him. At Abby's whimper, he took a calming breath. "It will be perfect for you. I promise," he breathed to her.

****

Geoff took his time washing up and dressing in one of the spare outfits he kept in his truck for emergencies. His head was spinning, and that was an unusual thing for a man that worked construction, even if your job *was* interiors, as his was.

Something had gone very wrong with Joey this morning, but he wasn't sure what. Logically, he'd digested that whatever it was hadn't stemmed from the sex of the night before.

It was the room...the bassinette. But that made no sense. The room had been largely cleared of what he'd assume were Jeremy and Alison's personal effects, so it wasn't being kept as a shrine.

Why would the bassinette bother him? If he'd learned one thing about Joey, it was that he had the most outrageous imagination, which made him the world's most protective daddy—biological father to Abby though he wasn't. *What scares him about a bassinette?*

He smiled grimly, his fresh t-shirt halfway over his head.

Knowing Joey, it could be nearly anything. *Oh well...one more thing to humor him about.* It never helped to try to work logic on Joey's latest fixation, and since it wouldn't hurt Abby to let him be overprotective—for now—Geoff was more than willing to let Joey get it out of his system.

His dirty clothing shoved in the duffel he'd removed from his truck the night before, Geoff stowed it in the nursery and made his way to the kitchen, savoring the scent of coffee rising up the stairwell.

Joey was at the table, feeding Abby rice cereal from a bottle designed to collapse as she swallowed mouthfuls of the new and exciting-to-her concoction. The baby bounced in a padded seat set into a metal frame. Her uncle had gone a step farther and clamped it to the table, so she couldn't overturn the seat as she grew. It was textbook Joey.

"Ah, where were those when I was feeding my daughter with spoons, and she was spitting it back at me?" He sighed at the improvements a few short decades had made.

Joey didn't crack a smile, as he usually would. "Coffee's ready," he announced.

"I see." Geoff went and got himself a mug of the potent brew—blond and bitter—and drank down a swig, wondering at Joey's attitude. "Look... If I overstepped the bounds by staying last night—"

"You didn't." But he didn't move to explain himself either. "Thanks for letting me sleep. I needed it."

"I think you need a few more nights of it."

"Probably."

"Joey—"

"Do you think Abby will react like your daughter did to learning I'm gay?"

The unexpected question shot a cold finger of fear down Geoff's spine. "You're not planning to get married to hide it from her or something like that, are you?"

"God, no!"

Geoff took a seat at the table. "Good. That's never a good idea. Then what are you thinking?" With Joey, you could never tell.

He seemed to consider his words carefully. "I don't want her to... You know."

"Well, I doubt that will happen unless you spend most of her life lying to her about it, like I did. If she grows up with you, knowing you're gay, I doubt it will be a problem for her."

Joey's shoulders eased, but his expression was still pensive and far away. "But she still won't have a female role model. Don't little girls need that?"

"Are you saying she needs a woman as a nanny?" There had to be a reason for this conversation, and Geoff was too muddled to find a logic string in it. *Is Joey trying to find a reason to get rid of me? If so, why would he*

42

Joey's brow furrowed. "Of course not. Where are you getting this stuff? A nanny isn't role model...usually. Maybe sometimes, I guess."

"Joey, you're not making sense. It'll be years before Abby needs a female role model, and when she does... Well, I'm sure you have some female friends, right?"

His cheeks darkened a few notches. "Yeah. I guess so."

"What's really bothering you? Why did the master bedroom—"

"I'd rather not talk about it." The answer had a bite that chilled Geoff.

"Sure. I won't use it again."

"I'd appreciate that." He sounded it, which only confused Geoff more.

Chapter Eight

The scream of a siren brought Geoff's gaze up to the rearview mirror. A fire engine was closing fast on him. He pulled to the right and stopped, clearing the way. It roared past him and toward the plume of smoke rising in the distance.

He sat there a long moment, staring at nothing in particular. How had he ended up here? A week ago, he would have sworn his life was close to perfect.

Last night, I would have opted for saying it was perfect.

That wasn't something Geoff wanted to consider. It was easier to count the blessings than obsess over a kid that was way too young for him and carried more baggage than any three of Geoff's prior lovers.

How would I know? I never got to know any of them well enough to see the baggage.

That was true enough. When Joey had showed up on his doorstep, Geoff had thought the young man's only problems were two obnoxious local punks. How little he'd known Joey then.

How little I know him now! Geoff tightened his fists around the steering wheel, frustrated almost as much by his lack of connection to Joey Biers as he was by the fact that he *wanted* to understand him better.

"Fuck this." There was no way he was going to solve the problem of Joey tonight. "So what's the plan?" he challenged himself.

Go home.

Get a hot shower.

Try to get a night of sleep.

Tackle Joey in the morning.

Hopefully, he'll be less raw then. Hopefully, he'll talk to me. Geoff hoped Joey would settle down and explain things coherently.

Joey had come home in no better a mood than he'd left in. That was the only reason Geoff had withdrawn instead of spending another night, as he'd originally planned.

He hoped more fervently that it wasn't over. Geoff loved Abby and... Well, he wasn't ready to say he loved Joey, but he was damned close to it.

That's a first. That was something Geoff had never said to a man before, even his own father. Rattled by the reality of the situation, he pulled onto the road and made his way home.

The acrid smell of smoke got thicker as Geoff approached home. He looked up at the billowing smoke, his mind working fast. The direction and distance told a tale Geoff didn't want to hear. He made the final turn, his heart stuttering at the sight of his house engulfed in flames.

Two pumper trucks poured thousands of gallons of water into the structure through broken and blackened windows. Two brave firemen stood on the roof, chopping holes in the shingles, tethered for safety.

A horn sounded behind him, and Geoff pulled his truck to the side, letting a police cruiser past, then put it in park. He slid out of the truck without turning it off and ambled across the street.

Flames shot through one of the holes in the roof, and the fireman on that side scrambled down. A shout went up, and one of the hoses angled up to pour water onto the conflagration.

Geoff looked from window to window, his mind spinning. All his precious belongings going up in flames marching through his mind, he sank to the grass.

Chattering voices drew closer. Geoff ignored them. His entire world was imploding. Whatever else was going on was of little consequence.

"Geoff! Oh, Geoff! You're all right." Tricia knelt beside him and wrapped her arms around his shoulders. "I saw your car through the garage windows, and I couldn't be sure which..." She sobbed.

He reached up and patted her hand awkwardly, at a loss for what he could possibly say. *It's all gone. Even the pictures of Ryssa are gone.* The only ones left were the two in his wallet.

"Mr Allread?" a gruff voice inquired.

"Yes. This is Geoff," Tricia answered for him.

That was a good thing. Geoff wasn't sure he was up to answering for himself.

"Mr Allread, do you have any idea who might have done this?"

That kicked his mouth and throat into gear. "It was set?"

No one answered, and Tricia's arms tightened minutely.

Geoff looked up at the police officer, noting his darkened face, his averted eyes. "Was it?"

His gaze flicked toward the house and away again. Geoff followed his line of sight.

It took a minute for the word painted in rust-brown paint to take shape through the soot and smoke. *Faggot.*

His jaw tightened down a notch. "Yeah. I do know someone that would do this." How many times had he mused that those two boys were going to get themselves into a world of trouble by doing something stupid?

Too many to count.

While he watched, flames from the closest window licked at the offensive slur.

Take it as a sign, Geoff. It's time to move on. Though he wasn't much for signs and portents, this latest fiasco was enough to make it through his disbelief.

****

Joey tilted the cereal bottle farther up, and Abby kicked her feet happily, curling her toes into fists and releasing them.

The silence of the house was unnerving. Only hours after he'd chased Geoff away with his foul mood, Joey missed the other man's company.

It's always like this. The hour or two Joey and Geoff overlapped at home were the highlight of his day. Work kept Joey busy enough not to obsess over Abby or anything else in his life. But the hours at home without the benefit of Geoff's company were empty and worrisome.

Joey sighed, looking up to meet Abby's avid inspection. His niece patted the side of the bottle. Though it was probably a random experiment in muscle motion, much as it was when she grabbed the spoon during feedings, it sounded like a demand to Joey.

"I'll apologize tomorrow, Abby. I promise."

As if she understood and approved, Abby kicked her feet and got the seat bouncing. Joey's laugh cut off at the sound of his cell phone ringing.

He fished it out and checked the number. It didn't register as someone in his phone book. Neither was it an 800 number, so he took the chance and opened the line.

"Hello?"

"I won't be in tomorrow."

"Geoff? What's wrong?" Something had to be to put that distressed tone in the gruff man's voice. "Are you okay?"

"I know I promised you two weeks, and I'll give you that. After that...maybe Tricia would be willing to—"

Joey's heart stuttered. "You found a new job?" He hadn't realized Geoff was looking for one. *I thought he was happy here.*

"I'm moving on, Joey. I'll give you the two—"

"You can't just move away. What about your house?" *What about us?*

"It burned."

"What?" Dozens of questions milled in Joey's mind.

"More precisely, it was burned down."

"Are they sure?" *Who would do that? Why would they?*

Geoff let loose a harsh laugh. "Based on the word painted on the front of the house, I would say—"

"*What* word?" His voice went up an octave, he was sure.

There was a moment of tense silence.

Joey calmed himself. "What word, Geoff?"

"Faggot."

Whatever his roiling mind would have spit out stuck in Joey's throat.

"I'm tired of being the old faggot on the block, Joey."

"And moving will change that? Are you planning on pretending to be straight again?"

He didn't answer the accusation.

"Geoff—"

"I'll go somewhere where no one knows me, Joey. I'll just be an aging divorced guy whose kid never visits."

"Sounds awfully lonely," he ground out.

"Yeah. Life sucks, right?"

"Maybe all you need are new neighbors."

"That's what I'm talking about," Geoff thundered.

"Ones that already know and like you, Geoff." His heart pounded a staccato beat.

Geoff's reply was weary...defeated. "What are you saying?"

"Move in here permanently. Become part of our family."

"Until I do the wrong thing again?" There was a bitter bite in that.

I deserve that one. "I'm sorry about that. I'd intended to tell you tomorrow, but—"

"Eventually, you'll find a guy your own age and—"

"I don't *want* a guy my own age, Geoff. I want you."

There was no reply to that.

"We've been practically living together for a month. We fit. You, me, and Abby."

Geoff sighed. "I'm too old for you, Joey. You're too set in your ways. It will never work."

"Where are you? Do you have a place to stay tonight? Come here. We'll talk. Not tonight, if you're too tired. Just... Just give us a chance."

"There's no place for me there, Joey. You know it, and I know it." But his voice said he wished that wasn't the case.

I hope.

Joey opened his mouth to protest, and the click of Geoff closing the line stopped him short. He stood there, numb, the phone pressed to his ear.

Abby's wail jump-started his mind again. Joey closed the cell phone and set it on the table. Then he unfastened the straps on the bouncy seat and lifted Abby out.

"I know," he soothed her. "We'll change Geoff's mind. I promise." But how he was going to do that was a mystery to him.

His niece rubbed her face on his shoulder, announcing that a crib trip was in her near future.

Not yet. I have to convince Geoff tonight. Joey didn't doubt Geoff would disappear if he gave him until tomorrow. Just because he'd promised to work the two weeks didn't mean he would.

That thought in mind, Joey picked up the cell phone, flipped it open, and pulled up the call history. A few clicks later, the phone was ringing.

"Midnight Motel," an annoyingly cheerful voice answered.

"Hi. I'm meeting a friend, and I need your street address for the GPS." *Well, it's half true.*

"Sure. No problem at all."

Joey smiled. *Time for a car ride, Abby.*

Chapter Nine

Joey's nerves jumped and shimmied as he passed by the motel office. It was certain they wouldn't tell him which room Geoff was in, so he didn't bother asking.

"Come on," he breathed. Joey scanned his gaze over the darkened parking lot through the sheen of rain. There weren't many vehicles, which meant chances were high that Geoff had parked right outside the door to his room.

What if he didn't? What if I wake someone up at nine at night?

I'll bluff my way out and apologize. For once, Joey didn't allow himself to obsess over the details.

He turned the corner to the back of the building and spotted Geoff's truck halfway down that side. It was parked at the door to one of the rooms. Whether it was the correct room remained to be seen.

****

Geoff paused in the process of towel drying his hair and shot a wary look at the door. Someone was knocking at this time of night?

I probably left my lights on when I stumbled in here after talking to the police and firemen. That will be the manager or one of the people in neighboring rooms telling me about it.

He scowled. *But only because it bothers them, of course.*

He strolled to the door, reached for the knob, then stopped short. In this neighborhood, it could be suicide to open the door blind. *And they still haven't found Mark and Taylor Jamison. They know my truck.*

Another knock startled him into motion, and Geoff eased the curtain aside to peek out. Before what he was seeing registered with his conscious mind, his subconscious was opening the door locks. Geoff dragged the door open and shot Joey a look he hoped conveyed that he was about to kick the young man's ass.

"What the hell were you thinking bringing Abby to this neighborhood?"

Joey shrugged, shifting his armload of sleeping baby slightly to accomplish the move. "You wouldn't come to us, so we're coming to you. If you don't like Abby being here, you can come home with us now."

Geoff glanced down at his body, numbly noting that the towel wrapped around his waist was all he was wearing. *At least I'm not hard enough for Joey to see it.* "Get in here, damn it." *It's better than leaving him standing in the rain with the baby.*

He moved a step aside and let them pass, then took his time to close and lock the door. At last he turned to look at them.

The sight of Joey stunned him. The lamplight glittered its way through the raindrops on Joey's golden curls, creating a halo around his angelic face.

He's so young. It never ceased to amaze Geoff how young Joey looked.

"I'm sorry," Joey whispered. "I'll explain it all, if you want. Maybe you can help me with what I need...want to do for Abby. I'll... I won't act that way again. I'll try my best not to. I can't promise I'll be perfect, I know, but—"

Geoff shook his head. "It's not that easy, Joey. You can't just change what you are to try and make a

52

relationship work. I know that. It's the beginning of the end."

"You were lying to your family about what you are. I'm just a little neurotic, and I fully admit it. I didn't say I was going to change that. I said I would explain it instead of blowing up at you."

Answering that was difficult. It was blunt and far too true. Geoff forced an answer out anyway. "I'm still too old for you. I can't change that. We have to face the facts."

"Who says?" Joey challenged.

"The laws of nature, last time I checked. You can't turn back the clock...or speed it up."

"No. Who says you're too old for me? I can name plenty of couples where one of them was three times the age of the other. Hell, you're not even twice my age." He stared at Geoff, waiting for a rebuttal.

It seemed impossible to formulate one.

Joey's expression softened. "Abby misses you already. I miss you. Gone an hour, and I miss you. Can you honestly say you wouldn't miss us too?"

I would, damn it. Admitting that was more than Geoff could bear.

"Just give it a try," Joey pleaded. "Just give *us* a try."

Us. That was so tempting. *Don't make promises you might not be wise to keep. Or able to keep.* "Two weeks. We'll try it for two weeks." *The two weeks I've already promised him.*

Joey paled a notch, then nodded.

"Now get that baby back to her crib," he ordered.

"Not without you." His stubborn streak was showing. "You stay, we stay."

As if punctuating that statement, lightning struck. *Close.*

53

Joey smirked. "Sounds like the weather isn't safe for driving. I guess we're all staying, like it or not. Or do you want me to get a second room?"

"Smart ass. You know I don't want that."

"I'm sure we can find somewhere for Abby to sleep." He glanced around, seemingly at a loss to offer a suggestion for it, despite his bravado.

Geoff sighed and strode to the dresser. He pulled one of the deep bottom drawers out and considered it. Joey wouldn't want to put it on top of the dresser or the table; he'd likely envision Abby knocking it off and hurting herself. He settled it next to the bed instead.

Joey eyed it warily. Just when Geoff became convinced he'd balk, Joey cleared his throat and nodded. "That works, I suppose."

Maybe he wasn't a lost cause after all.

Epilogue

"You are absolutely insane," Geoff accused. *I didn't realize I was living with a madman.*

Joey laughed heartily. He had calmed considerably in the last few weeks.

Well, he is better rested now. That had to help. He was also getting more relaxed and at ease with taking care of Abby.

"I don't think I am. You've been saying 'two weeks' for the last fourteen weeks. You've been living here and sleeping in our bed all that time. You're making long-term plans to preserve Alison's room for Abby. How much longer are you going to drag this out?"

"I'm living here. I admit it," Geoff groused. "I don't intend on leaving anytime soon."

"Come on. Admit it."

Geoff sighed, exasperated with his young lover. Joey had a romantic streak a mile wide, a mushy side that Geoff had never appreciated until Joey came into his life. But that didn't mean Geoff was going to get mushy with him. Not a chance. "Pushy little bastard."

"Even Abby is learning to say it," Joey teased.

"Wub does not necessarily mean what you believe it does," he countered.

Joey shot him what Geoff was sure was a mock glare. "What I know it does, you mean?"

"Fine." Geoff leaned down and kissed Abby's cheek. "I wub you."

She clapped her hands and let loose her two-toothed smile. The Cheerio she'd had pinched between her thumb and forefinger went flying. "Wub. Wub."

"Smart shit," Joey grumbled, his expression abruptly sober.

Geoff straightened. "You and I need to clean up our acts. Abby is going to start repeating those words soon."

"Yeah. Yeah." Joey turned away, but not before Geoff saw disappointment clearly painted on his face.

His heart ached. He'd waited too long to say it. Geoff swallowed hard. "I wub you too, Joey."

He whirled around, wide-eyed. "You really mean that?"

"Yes, I do. I wub—I mean I love you." He had no idea why he'd had such a hard time saying it. Geoff could say anything to Joey, and it was certainly true.

Hell, Joey had said it weeks earlier.

The man in question smiled. "Then I still think it's a good idea."

In her highchair, Abby was oblivious to the gravity of this discussion. She sat, blonde head bowed, working diligently at picking up another Cheerio. Only one in ten made it into her mouth. Most of her nutrition still came in the form of spoon-fed strained foods and bottles.

And Joey demands that someone stay at Abby's side every moment she has access to solid foods, unlikely as it is that she'll choke to death.

"Geoff?"

He probably thinks I'm ignoring the subject. "This is a really big step."

"And it went poorly for you last time, but that was a sham. This would be real."

It was hard to argue with that. He'd married Claire, because that was what he'd been expected to do. They'd had Ryssa, because that's what married people did. Not that Geoff hadn't loved his daughter. He still did, but he'd had her for the wrong reasons.

Joey shrugged, looking uncertain. "Look. It's simple and it solves all our problems."

"All our—"

"Okay. Several problems," he conceded. "Marry me. Before your medical insurance from unemployment runs out, you'll be covered by mine. We both adopt Abby. If anything happens to either of us—"

"And the house," Geoff parroted the practical concerns Joey had outlined earlier. He paused and then sighed. "Give me two weeks to think about it?"

"You and your two weeks. Some days I swear you are more afraid of change than I—"

"Da-da!"

Both of them swiveled their heads to look down at Abby. Geoff's mind spun at her outburst. She stared up at them calmly.

"She didn't just..." Joey whispered.

"Probably not." But it was nothing like her babbling sounds, and Ryssa had picked up that word—*Don't think about that.* "Maybe. It could have been. Let's see if she—"

"Da-da."

Repeats it. "Yeah. I think she did."

Abby cocked her head to one side and waited for something nameless.

"Which one of us do you think she's calling?" Joey asked. "Whichever one goes to her is going to be the one she thinks is Daddy. Isn't he? I don't want to confuse her, if she's already decided one of us is."

Typical Joey. He's overthinking this.

As if in answer to Joey's initial question, one chubby hand came out toward each of them, opening and shutting in the universal baby 'gimme' sign. "Da-da. Da-DA!"

That was clear enough. "I've thought about it," Geoff announced.

Joey shot him a look of confusion. "What?"

"The answer is 'yes'."

He gaped at Geoff, seemingly stunned.

"Who could deny that sweet face?"

Before Joey could more than shift his eyes toward Abby, Geoff captured his lips in a searing kiss.

Moments later, they broke apart. Geoff's cock strained the front of his jeans. "*Your* sweet face," he qualified.

"Pushover," Joey gasped.

Abby let out a happy squeal and clapped her hands awkwardly. "Da-da. Wub. Wub."

Joey laughed. "Yes, Abby. Your daddies do love each other. And you."

The End

About the Author

Brenna Lyons wears many hats, sometimes all on the same day: former president of EPIC, author of more than 100 published works, owner of Fireborn Publishing, columnist, special needs teacher, wife, mother...and member in good standing of more than 60 writing advocacy groups.

In her first ten years published in novel-length, she's won 3 EPIC e-Book Awards (out of 15 finalists) and finaled for 3 PEARLS (including one Honorable Mention, second to NY Times Bestseller Angela Knight), 2 CAPAS, and a Dream Realm Award. She's also taken Spinetingler's Book of the Year for 2007.

Brenna writes in 26 established worlds plus stand-alones, poetry, articles and essays. She's a bestseller in indie/e fantasy and horror, straight genre and cross-genres thereof. Brenna has been termed "one of the most deviant erotic minds in the publishing world...not for the weak." (Rachelle for Fallen Angels Reviews) Milieu-heavy dark work is practically Brenna's calling card, with or without the erotic content.

She teaches classes in everything from POV studies to advanced editing, networking to marketing. Brenna enjoys hearing from people who read her work and can be reached by e-mail.

Website: http://www.brennalyons.com/

Facebook: http://www.facebook.com/brenna.lyons

Email: brennalyons4168@live.com

Also by this Author

Maher Men
The Blutjagdfrau Chronicles
Veriel's Tales I: Crossbearer Turned
Veriel's Tales II: Losing Regana

URBAN GRIMM
Catch Me, If You Can
Three Wishes
Temptation of Eve

WEREWOLF U
Werewolf U
Younger Daughter
Alpha Son
Never Alone
Her Christmas Wolves

ANGEL-WING SAGA
Sons of Heaven: Beldon
Sons of Heaven: Unexpected Mates
Daughters of Man: Prize Match
Daughters of Man: Claiming a Princess

COLOR OF LOVE
The Color of Love

KEGIN SERIES
Conquest
The Last of Fion's Daughters
Last Chance for Love
Rites of Mating
In Her Ladyship's Service
Matchmaker's Misery

KIELAN SERIES
The Lady's Lowborn Lover
Time Currents
Cubed

STAR MAGES
Written in the Stars

The Master's Lover

DAN AIDAN FAIRIES
Fairy Dreams
Monsters of Myth Anthology

XXAN WAR
Daahan Rising
Raashh Decisions

MYTHOS SERIES
The Punishment of Phoebus Apollo
Black Sail

IT'S ALL GREEK TO ME...
All's Fair...

SANCTUM
Dream Walk

GRELLAN WAR
With Great Power

BLOOD MAGES
Enslaved

CARSON COUSINS
All I Want for Christmas is You

FATES WAR
Fates Magic

Beyond the Veil
Mine for the Night
Once in a Blue Moon
Overtime Pay
Stay With Me
The Fire God's Woman
Nevermore
Bride Ball
Undead in Blue

Mama's Tales
Unexpected Daddy
We Shall Live Again
May the Best Man Win
Marked
And It Was Good
Monsters of Myth Anthology

Available from **Under The Moon**

Evil Overlords Union Issue #1 Anthology
Undead Embrace
"Playing Games" in *Forbidden Love: Bad Boys*
"Marked" in *Forbidden Love: Wicked Women*
"The Master's Lover" in *Forbidden Love: Sacred Bands*

Available from **Logical Lust**

"Mine for the Night" in *The Cougar Book* Anthology

Available from **Coming Together Charity Anthologies**

INSTINCT SERIES
"Foundling" in *Coming Together: Into the Light* Anthology

"Claim Mate" (available separately and as part of the *Coming Together: Against the Odds* Anthology)
"The Fire God's Woman" in *Coming Together: Under Fire* Anthology

Available **self-published**

Snapshots from a Poet's Life

Award-Winning Books

EPPIE/EPIC eBOOK AWARDS WINNERS
Coming Together: Against the Odds- 2010
Time Currents- 2010
Coming Together: Into the Light- 2011

EPPIE/EPIC eBOOK AWARDS FINALISTS
Fion's Daughter- 2004
Collected Poems: Book One- 2005 (now titled *Snapshots of a Poet's Life*)
Renegade's Run- 2005
Rites of Mating- 2006
All I Want for Christmas- 2006
Phaze in Verse- 2008
"The Fire God's Woman" in Coming Together: Under Fire- 2009
Three Wishes- 2010
Matchmaker's Misery- 2010
The Cougar Book- 2011
The Master's Lover- 2011
Bride Ball- 2011

DREAM REALM AWARDS FINALIST
Last Chance for Love- 2003

PEARL HONORABLE MENTION
Night Warriors- 2004

PEARL FINALISTS
Schente Night- 2003 (now included in *The Last of Fion's Daughters*)
König Cursebreakers- 2004 (now titled *Will of the Stone*)

JOYFULLY REVIEWED BEST BOOKS OF 2010
Written in the Stars- 2010

SPINETINGLER'S BOOK OF THE YEAR 2007

NOBODY: An Anthology of Dark Fiction- 2007 (Brenna's pieces of the anthology can be found in *Beyond the Veil*)

TRS's CAPA FINALISTS
Ultimate Warriors- 2004 (Brenna's portion is now available as *With Great Power*)
Written in the Stars

LOVE ROMANCE AND MORE CAFÉ BOOK OF THE YEAR RUNNER UP
Last Chance for Love- 2008

ROAD TO ROMANCE REVIEWERS' CHOICE AWARD
Prophecy: Revelations- 2004

LOVE ROMANCES REVIEWERS' CHOICE AWARD
Black Sail- 2003

ROMANCE JUNKIES BOOK CLUB STAFF PICK
TYGERS- 2003

FALLEN ANGELS ROMANCE RECOMMENDED READ
*Devon's Price-*2005 (now available in *Bearing Armen*)

JOYFULLY RECOMMENDED READ
Fairy Dreams- 2008
The Last of Fion's Daughters- 2009

TREBLE HEART FINALIST
Prophecy: Revelations- 2003